THE MOUNTAIN MEN'S UNTAMED BRAT

WILD AND RECKLESS

DOVE PRIEST

First Edition

EBOOK ISBN 978-1-923471-84-9

PRINT ISBN 978-1-923471-21-4

Eden Jane has been our Achille's Heel for years. Now she's back and we can't choose who'll have her.

MY BEST FRIEND'S GIRL. The brat I've wanted but could never have.

That's who Eden Jane has always been to me.

Untouchable.

Off limits.

THE DAY EDEN turns up on the doorstep of Winterfox Wood Ranch three years after she walked away, looking pretty as sin and tasting like honey, I know all the promises that we made to each other are done.

Me, Beau and Sawyer.

This place bears my name as well as theirs. Which means that now Eden's back, she's fair game. But what if she wants more? What if she wants...all of us? I know we all need her.

Beau can push Eden away all he wants, but if she happens to fall into my arms one night during a camping trip, I won't turn her away. Neither will Sawyer.

If Beau wants to claim her, he'll have to leave the

1

ranch house he's hidden away in since she left him last time, begging on his knees for her to stay.

I know he'll kneel for her again.

And I can almost bet she'll brat it up for all of us.

Good. Because that's my favorite game.

THE MOUNTAIN MEN'S UNTAMED BRAT is a spicy, second chance why-choose romance where the heroine isn't the only one who gets some action, and the side character becomes the main character.

.

Read the men of WILD AND RECKLESS, where the romance is spicy, and the women never have to choose their love interests across three stunning authors

CHAPTER ONE

EDEN

Winterfox Woods Ranch is where my innocence died one perfect summer three years ago. *Will this time be different?* That's the definition of insanity, right—repeating the same experiment over and over and expecting a new outcome?

Back then I was a kid, hence the innocence factor. Beau Hansen certainly wasn't. He knew exactly what he was doing when he asked me out after graduation, before I left for college. Back when I had dreams in my eyes bigger than any small town could ever fit.

Back when one of the heirs of Winterfox was the

best thing that could happen to me at the freest time in my life.

And the worst.

The ranch hasn't changed, even if I have. A long dirt drive, neatly graded, leads to the peaked roof homestead tucked away in the heart of Winterfox Wood. The veranda wraps around the entire house that's shaded by a dense thicket of young spruce trees. I frown. The trees are way too close to the house, and Hank Hansen should know that.

Wildfire is a real risk out here, especially with summer and warm nights setting in. I pick up my pace, hoisting my bag higher on my shoulder. The straps dig into my skin, but I ignore the pressure. The house isn't that far away, and then I can stop.

Three families own the land that sits in a valley between two tall mountains no one else ever ventures between: Winters, Fox, and Hansen. The first two families moved away a few years ago. One when Mrs. Winters left abruptly, and shortly afterwards the Winters moved to another piece of land they own, closer to where their daughter lives. California, I think? I'm so out of touch with what's happened back home. Well, here. Larsen's Peak, the nearest small town. NYU is a long way from where I've spent the last three years of my life.

But it's Hank Hansen I'm praying will take me in

today. My own family is gone, and I've got nowhere left to go. The trip back here—home, whatever—has cost me everything.

Okay, not quite everything, but close enough.

That version of me, the girl who stood here last dressed in a threadbare cotton dress? She tucked her scholarship away as her *get out of small town hell free* card. And she waited on a man who *might* offer her the contradiction she craved: stability. Maybe even love. A schoolgirl's dream perhaps, but back then that's all I wanted.

It sure as fuck wasn't what I got.

I halt at the bottom of the steps to the homestead, unwilling to put my feet on the first wooden step. Because somehow that makes this whole thing more *real*. More than walking away from after I earned my fine arts degree at NYU. Then the hellish, sleepless trip back to Montana.

What brought me here, instead of the house I grew up in fifteen miles away. The keys sit at the bottom of my bag, untouched in three years.

I can't face that right now, so Winterfox Woods was simplest, the next best-worst decision I could make.

But I still can't force my feet onto that first step at the base of the homestead.

I lick my lips, staring at the closed door like I can

will it open. *Maybe he's not here.* Wait. That door was never shut. But someone was always home. That was one of the reasons Winterfox was my favorite place. Warm bodies filled the homestead no matter the season. Cody, Swayer...even Beau. Their sisters, parents during the season. Winter holidays together. Eating around the big table.

Playing hooky with Sawyer when Beau was too busy. Sneaking out to try Cody's newest batch of moonshine... My first kiss with Beau behind the bunkhouse that turned into a summer of kisses and so much more.

The memories I've tried to hide from myself assail me in a wave I can't stop.

I glance around again, shaking past ghosts away. Everything *looks* the same, but it isn't. Horses whicker quietly behind me, but I can't see a Winterfox branded cow in sight. Even the trees look older, the shadows between them darker.

The ranch has a distinct sense of stillness that's settled over the land, a haunting note that glides around me like a cool breeze trying to break up the summer heat, only there isn't one.

The ranch is deserted.

"Hank?" I yell, though I know better to expect an answer. My bag falls from my shoulder, a jangle of keys deep within that I ignore. Something so much worse than disquiet roils inside my stomach. *I should have called.* "Hank!"

I take the steps two at a time, banging on the screen door with my fist. I fully expect the screen to pop open and slap me in the face, or one of the boys to berate me from the other side for being too loud, yelling over me in bigger voices for shits and giggles.

Nothing.

I yank at the screen door, prepared to do battle with whatever has happened in this place in my absence, and nearly land on my ass.

It's locked.

I stumble backwards and crash into something warm. A shriek builds in my chest. *Bear. I wasn't watching, no one's home and I'm about to be mauled to death by a freaking bear—*

"Eden? What are you doing here?"

A bear who knows my name.

I pivot slowly on my heel, rolling my shoulders back and pretend I didn't just hide my face in my hands. A tall, blond cowboy with long hair that hangs over his face stands behind me like I didn't just try to run him over in my frantic retreat. An easy smile adorns his face.

"Hi, Cody." I dust my hands at my sides. "I was hoping Hank was in. I wanted to—"

Say hi. Beg a job from your pseudo-uncle. A place to sleep?

"He's not here." Cody's smile fades.

"Oh." I fidget and wish I hadn't dropped my bag that rests several feet behind him in the dirt. "It's just you, then?"

Cody glances behind himself. "You home for the holidays? I heard what happened to your parents. Have you been back to the house?"

"I don't want to talk about it," I cut him off abruptly and wince. "I'm sorry, that was rude," I mutter, studying my tattered trainers. His boots, new if a bit dirty, stand toe to toe with mine.

"'S'okay," Cody murmurs.

His hand, large and rough, finds my elbow. He pulls me into a hug that's all too easy to fall into. I resist for a second, but he's having none of it. Warm arms fold around me as I crash into his chest. There's a well that's been closed for far too long and in this place, with this man, who used to be a boy who chased me and played games and flirted harmlessly—suddenly, it's too much.

The well opens, and a sob rips free.

"Shit, girl. I'm sorry." Cody strokes my hair. He never lets go, and he never backs away. The cowboy just stands there, resolute as the torrents come crashing out.

Finally, my tears stop. I can't even say why in case it all starts again. "I'm sorry," I whisper, my breaths still ragged.

"It's okay." Cody doesn't sound like he's repeating himself as he holds me close. It's not invasive, his touch but easy, like him. "I'm glad you came here, instead of going there." I nod, glad he doesn't say the H word—*home*—unable to say much else. He seems to get it. The strong arms wrapped around me squeeze gently. "It's been a long time, Eden. I thought he scared you off."

Neither of us need to say which *he* Cody is talking about.

I shake my head the slightest amount. "Never," I whisper through cracked lips. "This is Winterfox Woods. It's always like—"

"Home," Cody finishes for me when I can't.

There it is. The word I've avoided for so long.

I nod. "Yeah," I manage, my voice less than a whisper as his forehead brushes mine in the barest touch. Pressure, nothing more. Cody angles his head, his mouth a breath from mine.

My heart beat ratchets up the pace, five beats too fast. *This isn't what I came here for!*

Isn't it?

"Are you here alone?" The words blurt from my

lips before I have a chance to take them back, ruining the moment.

Cody eases back, his mouth open to answer me, but it's not his words I hear.

"No. He's not."

Good feelings gone.

Beau Hansen's harsh voice is undeniable. I stiffen in Cody's arms that tighten on my back. He swears softly as I look up, knowing my apology is written on my face. Something different wars across his face in a breath of a moment. Anger, maybe. *Regret.*

Cody's hands fall from my arms as I increase the distance between us and pivot to face the bear waiting inside the house.

It's Hank Hansen that I came to see, but his son is the spitting image of him, maybe thirty years younger. Beau looks almost exactly the same as he did when I left him standing right where he is now, on the threshold to the ranch house to Winterfox Woods ranch house when I walked away from him last time.

Then, he was the one begging me to stay and I was the one leaving. Now when the roles are reversed, and I'm the one begging for a bed, my stomach swoops.

I lick my lips, then berate myself for giving him

any show of nerves. Beau misses nothing. He never did. I doubt that has changed. He's always been sharp, especially when it comes to me. I want to back up a step and hide in Cody's easy warmth, but I have to deal with the hot mess before me. It might as well be now.

And oh, what a hot mess it is.

Black hair lies tousled across his forehead, cut slightly shorter than it used to be. Deep blue eyes pierce straight through me. It feels like Beau is intent on excavating every single secret of mine that he can uncover in the space of thirty seconds or less. Not that I have many. Just one, and it's not really mine to tell.

His dark blue shirt sits tight across the hard line of his shoulders. The cotton is tucked neatly into his jeans. Fresh boots sit on his feet. All the signs that the ranch—and the boys—are doing well despite the obvious lack of staff.

I blink. "Sawyer. Is he around too?" I have a million questions, and that's the one that falls out. It makes sense. If the older generation have all left, then that's who must run the ranch now: Cody Fox, Sawyer Winters, and Beau Hansen.

Just because that last doesn't have his name to Winterfox Woods doesn't make the land any less his.

Beau freezes, reaching for me.

Damnit, I should have kept my mouth shut.

His gaze cuts away from mine, connecting with Cody's over my head, completely locking me out. "If she needs a place to stay, the bunkhouse is made up. She can stay there. Dinner's at—"

"Six. I remember." I refuse to be some discarded toy he thinks he can control and toss aside yet again just because I won't play by his rules this time around.

But I need him.

Damnit, I wanted to deal with Hank, not his son. We have too much of a history to make this work. But what did I think would happen? Ranching is in Beau's blood. It's in all of the boys. There's no world where we can exist and this ranch would be that they aren't on the land.

"Good." He glances down at my t-shirt and jean shorts, his gaze trailing over my legs and then back along my body to my face again. "Dress up, Eden. Dinner isn't...casual." Beau turns on his heel, disappearing into the shadows within the homestead.

"Good chat," I mutter under my breath.

"He's been like that ever since—" Cody cuts himself off.

I twist about and find him with my bag slung

over his shoulder. "I can take that." I hold out my hand, but he shakes his head.

"Come on, honey badger. I'll show you to the bunkhouse." A frown decorates his forehead for a moment before his expression smooths out.

I instantly hate that he's covering for Beau's bad humor. We both know there's plenty of bedrooms in the homestead, and one I used to stay in regularly before Beau and I were together. Unless something huge has changed, I can bet good money that old room still looks just like it used to when I last stayed there.

"Honey badger?" I raise both eyebrows, following him down the stairs. "That's a bit strong, don't you think?"

Cody flashes me the same easy grin from before. The one that nearly landed me a kiss within minutes of arriving. The one that Beau broke up.

"Sweet thing, if you think that I'm the least of your problems, wait until Sawyer sees you looking so fine. He's gonna shit bricks though when he finds out that Beau's hidden you away in the bunkhouse. Come on. I'll give you a tour."

I shake my head and take the outstretched hand he offers, hoping that Beau is watching and sees every flirtatious moment of Cody hamming it up for me even though I don't trust a word he says. Well, maybe one or two.

Sawyer will be pissed that Beau's shunted me out of the homestead for sure. There's some truth in that.

"I've been here before. You know that, right?"

"I know." Cody squeezes my hand. "But anything that gets you and me some time together I'll take, honey badger."

"Stop with the freaking honey badger shit already," I mutter, letting him lead me toward my new home for the foreseeable future.

Maybe coming back to Winterfox Woods is the worst idea I've had in ages. But then, Beau never told me to leave. He didn't really give me a choice. He's just sort of... put me out of sight, for a bit.

My lips twitch. *Well then, Mister Beau Hansen. Let's see if I can't rile you up a little while I'm here.*

Because if there's one thing I'm good at, it's bratting it up. Beau knows that damn well.

And from what I remember, he loves it.

CHAPTER TWO

BEAU

Eden Jane shouldn't be at Winterfox Woods. Not because she doesn't belong here—but because she *does*.

It's all too easy to remember the summer she spent here the last three years ago as I walk through the empty ranch house on my own. Only ghosts live here now. Memories of the months we shared together before she left to create a life states away. Now, the windows are closed as always, curtains drawn. No light or air filters in the way it used to when she was here.

Before everything changed.

She's back now, all bright and full of the same sass that used to drive me insane. My hands itch to dive through her hair, shove her against the wall and berate her for ever coming back. Or pull her against me and show her what her leaving cost me. What I'll do to keep her here every last second.

Which is why she can't stay in the house with me, or Cody, or Sawyer. Hell, I saw the way his hands were already all over her. She's too sweet and sassy for any of us. I know the lash of her tongue—in the air around me, in my mouth, on my cock.

Fuck, I'm hard just thinking about pushing her to her knees and filling her pretty little mouth until she's stuffed full and choking. Eden loves to suffer with her throat full, and tears in her eyes. Even with that cheery little facade on the outside, it never shows how broken she is on the inside. Hell, my favorite thing was always to watch her cum hands free at the same time as I poured myself down her throat, her orgasm slamming her simply from the depravity of our actions.

Or watching her struggle and not blow down her throat was our favorite form of torture, denial being a shared kink for us both.

But last time I begged her to stay, she walked away from me, intent on starting her own life far from Winterfox. It wasn't only my heart she shattered that day, and it fucking well hurt. If I let her into this house again and she touches me, I won't have the resolve to tell her to leave.

Hell, if she comes into the house and I let her touch me, she'll be back in my bed before I can think.

And if I do, I'll never let her leave.

CHAPTER THREE

SAWYER

The soft voice reaches me before my brain catches up with the new program at Winterfox Woods. It's been so long since we've had anyone else at the ranch, apart from a few seasonal hands to help out, that I'm used to being lost in my head for hours each day. And let's be honest, with Beau's shitty attitude, those fresh hires never last long.

It's like I've forgotten what a woman's voice sounds like out here, so the sight of Eden chatting and flirting her perfect as fuck ass off in those too-short denim cut off short floors me.

"Look who showed up," Cody greets me with a grin.

I stare at the vision of the goddess before me. All tanned legs I swear run for miles, and honey blonde hair that hangs in waves over her shoulders. In the last few years, Eden's developed extra curves that she didn't have the last time she was out here on ranch land fucking the shit out of my best friend. I swallow hard and try not to gawk at the way her breasts strain against her thin, gray t-shirt, forcing my gaze to her dark brown eyes instead. There are flecks of gold there, like summer sunshine.

Yeah, I'm a real romantic.

Get your shit together, Winters.

I never touched her back then, when she was with Beau before. Eden was my best friend's girl. That meant she was off limits. *Fucking always.* But from the way she's hanging off Cody right now and how his hands are all over her? Apparently the game changed while I was head deep in a pile of cow dung and she grew up in another state without us.

"What are you doing back here?" Yeah, I'm all approachable and shit.

That's what happens with me and a pretty girl who has to be, what, twenty-two, now? Something like that. She was always a few years younger than me and Beau, about the same age as Cody. I glare at him over her head while she chatters on, oblivious.

"I finished studying. Art." Eden turns back to

face me, tucking her chin as she leans against Cody, as though she's seeking his protection.

Shit. I scared her.

Cody frowns at me over her head. "Beau already sent her to the bunkhouse to sleep," he says pointedly. "I was taking her for a tour."

"Eden doesn't need a tour." I look between them both. "You practically lived here for a summer while you and Beau—" My mouth runs on while my brain belatedly plays catch up. "Wait, the bunkhouse?"

"Yeah." Eden draws circles in the dust in trainers that look like they're about to fall apart on her feet.

"Fuck that." I throw my shovel into the literal shitpile I've been working. "Beau can go suck on a bull's cock," I mutter furiously. My next glare is sent to Cody. "Sure, put her things in the bunkhouse, if you like. No one else is in it right now. But she's not staying there."

"Sawyer—" Eden starts to object, but I wave her down.

I might be covered in fuck knows what, but he's not treating her like this. Not when we're seeing her for the first time in years and—

Fuck. She's as broken as we are.

It doesn't take a genius to see that she's turned up on our literal doorstep in rags. I'll bet my share of the ranch that what's in the bag Cody's carrying over his shoulder is everything she owns apart from her parent's abandoned house a few miles away. She's got nothing, she didn't go home, and now she's here.

And he puts her in the bunkhouse?

Fuck. Him.

Beau hasn't been the same since Hank died. Of all people, he should understand what she's lost. Turning her away at our front door isn't the answer.

"I need to get cleaned up." I meet her eyes. "Sorry I can't hug you, firefly. But right now, I don't smell so good."

She shrugs. "You smell just fine to me." Her chin rises, bright eyes fill with her old brand of defiance.

Yeah, she'll fit in here just fine.

Once we've broken through Beau's shitty attitude, maybe. However long his moping takes to cure with her brand of brattiness.

"He stinks, honey badger." Cody leans down to whisper in her ear, loud enough for me to hear. She shivers as he rests one hand on her waist.

I watch their interaction, my mouth dry. *So that's how it is, huh?* Looks like Cody got in quick before me. But when Eden holds my gaze, hers flickering just a little at his touch, her sass and defiance is still there, along with a decent dose of heat.

You little brat. You want it all.

Or maybe she just wants to shit Beau off. Not the best plan, but even if he tries to throw her off Winterfox land, there's no chance in hell I'll let him, no matter who she's with, or none of us at all. Cody either, from the way his hands wrap possessively around her tight little waist, running over those curves I'll salivate over later.

"Firefly, I'm gonna go clean up. Cause even if you can't tell I smell like the wrong end of a cow, and not the pretty part. Then, we're gonna take you camping."

Cody grins, coiling his fingers through her hair to tug her face up to his. Her lips part, her thick lashes fluttering. "Remember the river, sweet thing? There's a field just beyond that where we can stay the night."

She fidgets, and it's cute as all fuck. "I don't have a tent or anything."

From the way Cody grins down at her like she's first snow on Christmas fucking morning, we won't have a problem in that department. "It's summer, sweet thing. No tents required. A fire will keep the nasties away. And you have us."

"A fire?" She looks up at me, nibbling her lip. It pops out and I bite back a groan. "What about—" She cuts her own words off and glances back toward the house.

I cover her slip smoothly. "Like Cody said. We have a fire to keep the nasties away. Fifteen minutes, firefly. I'll change and grab some food. Then we're gonna look after you tonight." I hold Cody's gaze while she studies the back of the house like she expects Beau to come storming out to stop us.

He won't. He's been hiding back there for far too long.

Cody meets my eyes, gives me a slow nod of his own. His fingers find her hip bone where he squeezes gently, just enough to draw a soft breath from her, in case the three of us aren't clear on the intent of the camping trip.

Eden leans back against Cody's taller frame, nestling against him like she's always belonged with him, and looks straight at me. "I can't wait."

Well, fuck me. Looks like one of us gets my best friend's girl after all. But screw Cody if he thinks I'll roll over and die while he stakes his claim on her without a challenge.

Beau can go sulk in the ranch house for as long as he likes. I have a camping trip to organize.

CHAPTER FOUR

EDEN

Cody leans against the doorway to the bunkhouse, watching me unpack my things. No matter what Sawyer says, I can't force myself to go into the homestead, or face Beau. If he doesn't want me there, then this is where I'll stay. I'm stubborn, I know, but then that's how we've always been. Me, fighting back against the invisible force that's him. Besides, I need a place to stay. If Beau throws me out, then I'll go. Then there's only one place left I have to hide away from the world.

And I don't want to go there alone.

Cody's attention on me is blistering hot. I use

my hair to hide from him as I unpack my text books and a handful of books with worn covers. He whistles.

"What?" The single syllable comes out defensive.

"I mean, if I knew that's what you were into I would have sent you book dollars each Christmas, honey badger." He saunters into the bunkhouse, breaking the invisible barrier between us.

"You–there." I point. "Stay. Go," I flap my hands at him. "Out! My space."

Cody puts on a wounded face as he picks up my collection of historical romances. Okay, fine. They're bodice rippers with the obligatory regency hero depicted on the cover with a busty heroine draped over his arm. Breast tumble everywhere, much more than I'll ever be blessed to have. I cross my arms over my own chest and kick my Viking subtly romance under one empty bunk.

"You want space, Eden?" Cody steps closer, his fingertips lingering on the book covers as he leans into my breathable area. All the air disappears in an instant. "Are you sure that's what you want?" He takes that same hand and drags it along my spine.

"I—" Words fail me. His touch is everything. I swallow and try to focus. *Not on him.* Not yet.

Tonight. "Do I need a sweater?" I force my face up to his in some semblance of an innocent expression. Not that I have one, but he doesn't need to know that.

Cody's pupils dilate. "Christ, honey badger. Look at me like that tonight, and I won't be a responsible adult."

"Cody Fox. You were *never* responsible, and who says you ever grew up to be an adult?" I twist away from him, dancing out of his grasp.

His hand shoots out to catch my wrist. "A lot of things changed while you were away, Eden," he growls, his voice low.

So low that all the hair stands up along my arms. Cody closes the short distance between us, reeling me back into him. His grip on my wrist gentles, the rough pad of his thumb tracing light circles over my pulse point.

"I can't breathe," I whisper as my heart beats too fast, knowing he can feel everything that I do.

Cody leans closer, his warmth eating up the space between us. "I'll breathe for you," he promises, tipping my face up to his.

"Ready to go." Sawyer's voice crashes into us the same time as he kicks the already open door to the bunkhouse.

Hard enough for the wood to bounce against the frame and nearly splinter.

I jump backwards, but Cody doesn't let me go. He only raises his head in acknowledgement of the timed interruption. He nods once as my heart slams in my ribs. I just got here and I swear I won't be able to take much more of these two. Maybe I should try my chances in the homestead with Beau?

"You heard the man." Cody squeezes my hip like he did earlier, only a little lower this time, his intent and possession clear. "Let's go, sweet thing."

I glance back at him, then to Sawyer.

Cody's usually easy smile is tainted with heat and desire. But Sawyer, when I refocus on him, dressed in a white tee beneath an open red checked shirt over his worn jeans and boots, looks more relaxed than when we met him working before.

I offer him a soft smile, my heart tugging in two directions at once, or maybe three.

Beau should be here.

"Come on, firefly." Sawyer holds out his hand as Cody nudges me forward. "Let us show you what's changed about Winterfox since you were here last."

Cody trails his fingers along my spine as I let them lead me from the bunkhouse.

"And what hasn't."

WINTERFOX WOODS DELVES DEEP into the valley behind the bunkhouse. Mountains rise either side of us, still on ranch land that divides us from the small towns on either side. The town I once called home. It was always one of the reasons I loved coming here, like I could hide away from the world, forget it existed.

Or be forgotten.

The river's rushing chatter reaches me well before I see the water as we walk, the boys flanking either side of me on the trail. No one talks, though hands brush mine occasionally. Those small touches are enough to ward away the doubts—of coming here, my future. The past.

Cody carries bedding on his back while Sawyer takes the food. They both refused to let me bring anything, making all the decisions for me. It's both sweet and infuriating at once.

Sawyer's glance over his shoulder as he leads us beneath the interlocking canopy is assessing and protective. He checks behind us yet again, but I know he doesn't expect to see anyone else back there. "Keep up, Eden," he murmurs more than once as we traipsed beneath the thick branches.

I brush my fingers over a twisted crab apple, its fruit long turned sour on tortured branches—more than one—as I pass. "I remember planting there. Years ago, when I was a kid. Wasn't it your sister, or Cody's who loved plants? I don't remember." Too many years have passed between now and then. "But I swear this area used to be more open."

Sawyer's step jolts. "Everything changed after you left." His voice roughens. "It's not just your family who—"

Cody coughs behind us, and Sawyer falls silent.

I can't tell if it's the rushing waters or the shadows that cool the air more, but gooseflesh bursts across my arms. I wrap my hands around my middle, breaking contact with the Winterfox boys.

"He's right. Things changed." Cody breaks into my thoughts.

I lick my lips, my mouth dry, and wonder how long I've been quiet for, lost in my head. Sawyer passes back a water bottle. I take his offering gratefully, mouthing *thank you*, though nothing comes out.

He nods and faces forward, forging onward.

"We lost Hank to cancer two years after you left," Cody continues at my back, talking like my brain is still functioning. Sawyer tenses up, his back as ramrod straight as one of the spruces that we pass. The behemoths guide our way along the thin path I don't think has been used by more than a few cows over the years.

"There's been changes for us all," I whisper, my voice loosened by a few home truths and the constant sound of water, as though it's part of our conversation too.

"Beau didn't cope well." Cody touches my elbow. "He's stayed in the house, done the accounts. We barely see him. He comes out to head to the sale-yards, keeps the same relationships going as always. But when he lost you–"

"Cody," Sawyer warns, his voice little more than a distant rumble despite that he's right in front of me.

"When you left Winterfox... this place has never been the same." Cody's chest presses to my back as dark shadows turn to light. The trees open out in front of us, dusky and purple with the falling evening. "We're here, honey badger. Like what you see?"

What I see is a seething Sawyer glaring over my head.

Cody's arm locks around my waist, warm and secure. "That way, Eden." He redirects my attention to the vista beyond the cranky cowboy in front of me.

My mouth falls open as I stare out at the field beyond the wall of foliage we've emerged from. Only, it's not just a field. A flattened patch of bright, soft grass is surrounded by a circle of giant larches. Beyond that, in one direction the mountain looms above us like a silent sentinel. On our other side, the ground slopes toward the river that rushes into a series of tiny waterfalls, one bouncing into the next. Then the water softens after the chaos, settling into a sweeping pool. My aching feet are desperate to submerge into the coolness.

Nope, it's not part of me. Just the whole of me.

"I'd like to see that." Sawyer drops his pack to the grass a few paces away. Apparently he's picked our spot for this trip.

I glance at him, distracted. "What? Wait, I said that?"

"Yeah, honey badger. That thought came out your mouth, nice and loud and clear." Cody tucks a curl behind my ear. His touch lingers on my throat, intimate and sensual.

My breath hitches as my gaze locks with Sawyer's. He swallows hard, hands fisting at his sides.

"I'll find firewood," he says abruptly, stalking away.

Cody laughs softly in my ear. "That boy doesn't know how to take what he wants." His fingers find my jaw and he turns me towards him.

"And you do?" The words are out of my mouth before I think them through.

"I do." His gaze is molten and hot and dark, and everything in my screams to either run or submit the moment he leans in.

This is *Cody Fox*. My ex's best friend, or one of them. Actually, I'm not sure where Cody sits in the pecking order at Winterfox Woods, between Beau Hansen and Sawyer Winters, but when his lips graze over mine, soft and sweet, I decide I don't care.

His pack falls to the ground with a thud, and those large, warm hands fold around my waist. But Cody doesn't rush me like Beau might. With him it was always a constant frenzy of tearing clothes and the sort of passion that, once ignited, can't be snuffed out. I bratted it up and he tried to tame me. Sometimes he succeeded. Sometimes I topped him and then paid for the privilege the next night. Sometimes he offered pleasure; other times, pain.

Cody Fox is nothing like that.

His kiss is liquid heat, languid and easy. I rock into his warmth, the protective circle of his arms safe and simple. He wants me, and I want him. No rules. No barriers. Those rough fingers tease the hem of my tee. I'm seconds from letting him take the material off over my head when a cleared throat pauses us both.

"Dinner first, okay?" Sawyer says pointedly. "Before I have to roll over and pretend not to listen to the pair of you fucking like bunnies for the night?"

My cheeks heat like volcanic rocks as Cody laughs, tucking me into his chest. "If you insist. Or we could fuck first, then eat?" His words are laced with innuendo as his knee presses between my thighs.

My groan turns into something a little more breathless. Sawyer stomps away again, muttering curses I can't decipher beneath his breath.

"Whaddya say, sweet thing? Wanna feed the beast before we tease him all night?" Cody kisses the corner of my mouth, his tongue flicking out to lick my lips, then he lets me go.

The cold void of where he was a moment ago hits me harder than if he had dropped me in the river.

"Damnit, Fox," I mutter. "You'd better be able to cook."

He throws me an impish grin over his shoulder.

"Are we making wagers? Because if we are, I can cook and make beds."

"Fuck off. If you're cooking, we'll all starve." Sawyer sets up a fire and casts a glance my way, shaking his head. Sandy blonde strands flick across his face. "Don't take any bets from this man, firefly. You'll end up regretting it."

I smother a giggle as Cody tosses me a blanket and a wounded expression, but I know he's only playing as Sawyer starts wrapping jacket potatoes in foil and corn cobs. I cast him a glance and settle on the bedroll that Cody helps me make up. I'm rusty, but these boys aren't. One thing niggles at me. I wait until Cody wanders into the trees, leaving me with Sawyer, then edge a little closer as darkness falls over us.

"I don't remember this place."

He doesn't glance up at me. "Winterfox is bigger than you ever knew."

"Is it?" I tip my head back to stare at the stars through the tip hole in the canopy between the larches. Some diamond pinpricks make it through the overlap above. "I thought I walked every inch of this land over time, apart from the mountains. Remember chasing the calves when they got out?"

Sawyer stiffens. "I remember."

"And that year when Cody got chicken pox? And

the girls? Your parents were so busy that no one else could help. The hands were sent away too, so you, Beau and I—

"*I remember,* Eden," Sawyer growls. He looks up at me across the fire, his face thrown into sharp relief. "I remember a whole lot more than you think."

CHAPTER FIVE

SAWYER

Damn, if Eden doesn't look so fucking beautiful sitting across the fire from me, curled on the pile of blankets that Cody made up for her like it's a freaking love nest. I can imagine him lying her back, covering her body with his heavier weight all too well, and making her moan until the sun rises tomorrow. Her scent is so honey sweet just beyond the tip of my tongue that if I strain, I can taste her. *Almost.*

Fuck, I'm sprouting a hard on already, and I'm growling after like a fucking beast. It's not even dinner time yet. *This isn't who I am.*

Isn't it?

When it comes to Eden Jane, this is *exactly* who I am.

"What do you remember?" she whispers, edging forward off her bedroll.

"Stop," I grate out, slamming my hand down on the ground beside where I'm cooking her dinner.

Eden freezes in place. She watches me like a deer caught in headlights. Then, very deliberately, she moves.

"Fuck," I grate out, raking my hand through my hair. It'll get grass and shit in it, but I don't care. If she touches me—

Her hand rests on my bicep. Heat ripples through me as I try to tame my breaths. "Why have you always hated me so much, Sawyer?"

I drop the utensils I'm working with and grip her waist. Soft flesh, the little of her that there is, dimples beneath my hands as I walk in a crouch to deport her back to her bedroll and dump her unceremoniously on the damn squishy thing.

"Stay. Here," I mutter, rising to tower over her. She gazes up at me, panting and sprawled out like I just tossed her away. Or threw her on the bed, ready for a damn good—

Ah, fuck.

I hightail it back to the fire, poking and prodding

at food that doesn't need assistance to cook unless I want it to die a speedy death.

"Sawyer?" Her soft voice breaks through my reverie. "I'm sorry. I didn't mean to upset you."

My eyes shutter. "I know, firefly. It's my fault. You didn't do anything."

She shifts, but doesn't approach me again. *Shit. I've scared her.* And who the hell wouldn't be scared? I just picked her up and threw her away for daring to touch me. My nails rake at the back of my neck over and over.

"You'll hurt yourself." Her soft words hit home harder than intended.

I huff a laugh. "My sister used to say the same thing."

"But she's not here now."

"No. She's not."

"No one is."

I hear the question in her unspoken words. *Where is everyone? What happened here?*

The same thing that happened to her, I suppose. People moved on. People died. We are the ones left behind still trying to keep it all going. Only she came here instead of going home. And look what we're doing to her. Cody's trying his damndest to seduce her. Beau refuses to speak to her. And me? I'm pushing her away with every word.

I close my eyes for a long moment, breathing in the scents of my cooking. It's one of those things that's always kept me sane. At the end of a long day knowing that I can make food for everyone left, provide one last service, that's when I know everyone's alright.

But it's not food I scent, or rather, it is. *Honey sweet.* Something I'd very much like to lick from the source.

I hold out my hand, rocking back onto my heels. "Come here, firefly," I murmur, steadying my breaths so I don't frighten her away again, panting after her like the beast in heat that I am.

Her touch, hesitant, leaves me rock hard and aching. I know she knows, because she presses her body to mine before I open my eyes.

I turn my head to look up at her where she stands beside me, tracing patterns I don't know across my shoulders. "I shouldn't have pushed you away."

Eden acknowledges my apology with a gentle tug to my hair. The strands have grown out, too long. They hang in pale dreads across my face. She brushes them aside. "Can I help you serve?"

I blink at her, and my breaths that I thought I had under control grow ragged. "Yeah, you can do that. Bowls are over there." I point to my collection of crap I've dragged with me from the house.

Her hands leave me. She digs about in my pack, coming back with what I need and some utensils. We work side by side in silence. Cody keeps his distance. His silhouette flitters about beyond the fire doing fuck knows what, but he gives us space, and I'm grateful.

"Better?" Eden places a bowl on my lap filled with salted corn, a quesadilla burned at the edges, and a jacket potato stuffed with ham, chilies and butter.

"Better." It takes everything I am not to discard the bowl and haul her onto my lap in its place. Pull her thin shirt aside and lick every inch of her skin. *Fuck. I'm so far gone for her.*

Keeping my hands off her while she and Cody get it on later is gonna be damn near impossible. I made a promise to myself earlier that I'd push for her, but if she's happy with him, who am I to fuck that up for her? The tease has already started as she licks her fingers and moans fucking loud as sin on a stick.

"That's so good, Sawyer."

"Firefly," I warn her, heat boiling low in my loins.

"What?" Her lashes fly wide as she looks at me

over three buttered fingers jammed in her mouth that she's still licking.

"Christ." I swear and look away.

Lie. I'm still staring at her like I wish those were my fingers jammed in her mouth that she's sucking on.

Cody jams his ass between us, grabbing a bowl. "Now you know why Beau's so fucking hung up about her, alright? She's a brat," he mutters out of the corner of his mouth.

I can't disagree with that. But Eden's a brat that I can't keep my eyes off as she sucks one finger at a time clean, her gaze locked on me the whole time. I swear I can feel those phantom lips gliding along my cock, the heat of her wet, warm mouth and tongue sucking away at my flesh—

"Fuck," I mumble, shoveling food into my mouth. Anything as a distraction from the show she's putting on.

The next laugh isn't Cody's. It's hers.

Eden knows exactly what she's doing. Maybe I should take a leaf out of Beau's book and spank the sass out of her.

Not that the strategy seems to have worked for him.

"Tell me why I can't remember this place?" Eden asks when we're through our meals.

Cody stays silent, sneaking a glance at me.

Guess I'm up.

I let out that same breath that seems like it's been lodged in my chest since she turned up on Winterfox Wood land again. "Beau never brought you out here, did he?" She shakes her head. "And we didn't either, back then." Another shake. I blow out a second breath. Time for a home truth. "Because you were his, then. Not ours."

Eden blinks.

"We all have our favorite places on the land, sweet thing." Cody pushes her bowl away and tangles their fingers together. My heart aches at the sight. "This is one of ours."

"Oh." The softest admission leaves her as she studies their laced hands. "How– how many women have you brought out here?"

Cody strokes her fingers. "You really want to know?"

"None." I put her out of her misery faster than he will. Eden looks up at me, gratitude filling her face. "We always wanted one girl we could—" The words stick in my throat. I can't force them out. "Give me your bowl and I'll clean up."

Cody collects everything, handing them over. He usually cleans if I cook but I think he gets that right

43

now I need time. And he doesn't seem like he's letting her go any time soon.

I shove the thought of them together out of my mind as I clean, ignoring the sounds of their chatter, cuddled together in the warmth of the fire's soft glow. I made it big enough that it'll carry us well into the cool of the night, not that we really need it for this time of year. It's there to look pretty, and to make Eden feel safe more than anything.

The only nasties we're keeping at bay tonight are the memories none of us want to face. Who we've lost. What she doesn't want to remember. Tomorrow we can deal with all of that, but it'll be together, not her alone. That's the promise we're making, even if I have to suffer through tonight on my own.

Her giggle when he kisses her neck. The sounds she makes, soft sighs as her body loosens, tension slipping from her, hurts me physically. My cock is still raging hard, but my chest grips my heart so tight I swear it'll fail the moment she moans for him.

I dry everything, walk the perimeter, and piss into the darkness, trying to shut out every single fucking soft sound when Cody kisses her. And when she's silent as I walk back to them, I can't help looking.

Her body is pressed flush to Cody's. Skin is on display in a thin strip across her back where her tee has ridden up. I catch a glimpse of sweet curves where her jean shorts sit low on her hips. My mouth waters at the sight. She's not the only one whose clothes are in a state of disarray before the fire. Cody's shirt is undone, and her mouth is latched to his chest in a series of tiny kisses. But her hands disappear into the front of his jeans.

His eyes roll back as she works him, biting his lips on the groans that so obviously try to escape.

I grab my pack, stuffing things into it, not caring if I'm loud or not. No matter how much I want her, I can't stay and listen to her give him pleasure all night. Not here, in the place where we promised that one day, if we ever got the chance to touch her, we'd share her.

It's the same reason we've never shared this place with anyone else.

Hell, as far as I know none of us have brought another woman back to the ranch in the last three years at all.

"Stay," Eden murmurs, glancing over her shoulder at me. She swivels in Cody's arms to face me. "Please, Sawyer?"

I stare at her, panting as his hands glide over the

curve of her stomach. "You can't ask me to stay and listen to—"

"Who says you just have to listen?" Cody's hands disappear under her shirt, cupping her breasts. He tugs and pulls, drawing moans from Eden. Her head tips back on his shoulder, her dark eyes shot with gold closing. He gives her a nudge. "Uh uh, sweet thing. Eyes open and on Sawyer if you want him to play with us."

My hard on thickens impossibly. "Eden?"

"Watch us?" she whispers, letting her hands fall to her sides. She makes no other protest as she lets my best friend play with her body the way he wants.

Fuck, it's the hottest thing I've ever seen.

Cody's grin is sly as he pulls her shirt up to expose her breasts. No fucking bra—when did she lose that? Or maybe she never had one on at all.

I toss my bedding back on the ground, letting my pack slip from my hands. Whatever willpower I had the slightest grasp on is long gone. I lie on my side, the fire slightly between us as Cody's fingers circle her nipples. The peaks are already stiff and engorged; even in the flickering light their color is a deeper purple than I expect, she's so needy already.

Eden's lips part on a cry as Cody pushes his knee between her legs. Her thighs fall open like her lips, the tip of her pink tongue emerging.

It takes everything I have not to reach into my jeans and rub one out, but I force my hands away from my dick, letting the ache, the tainted need of her consume me.

Eden grips the blanket beneath her, reaching back to fist Cody's shirt as he milks her nipples gently and sucks at her neck. She'll be covered in his marks by the time we get home. Beau will know we fucked with her and he'll be furious.

Maybe he should have come with us and shared his little toy around.

"Can you come from nipple stim alone?" Cody tugs her nipples a little harder, then backs off, leaving her on edge.

Eden shakes her head still moaning, then shrugs.

Cody laughs. "Why don't you unbutton your shorts and show Sawyer what color panties you're wearing? I bet you're soaked right through." He nuzzles at her ear as she moans.

Her eyes fly wide open and she shakes her head. "No," she whispers, her voice cracking.

"No?" Cody murmurs, amusement coating his voice as he rubs his body against hers. His thumbs circle her nipples, stroke beneath but he doesn't touch her.

Eden fucking *pants*. Her mouth opens, her

tongue slipping out on a moan. I want to slide my tongue inside and taste her, swirl it around and see if she'll rub her body against my cock.

Fuck, this is impossible. I'm so on edge that I'll come in my pants in seconds just watching them without touching myself at all.

Cody grazes his fingertips across her nipples then dives a hand straight down the front of Eden's shorts.

She screams, her eyes rolling back as she arches for him.

"Tell him why you won't undo your shorts and show him," he commands.

Eden shakes her head. "No–"

"Tell him what a perfect little sweet thing you are for us, Eden," Cody purrs, playing with her out of my sight.

"Fuck," I groan, reaching for my cock. I can't hold back. I can't.

"Tell him that you rode all the way from NYU and to our door without a single pair of panties in that suitcase of yours or on your tight as fuck little body, honey badger. Tell my best friend why I've got my fingers buried in your dripping snatch right now while he watches."

I stare, mesmerized at the bulge of Cody's

knuckles tenting the front of her denim shorts as he toys with her.

"Tell us who you were going to fuck at Winterfox Woods with this bare little cunt, Eden Jane."

CHAPTER SIX

CODY

Eden soaks my hand while Sawyer watches us with a tight expression like he's actually in pain. White dreads hang across his face, leaving him looking feral in the reflected light from the fire. I wonder how long he'll hold out before he either blows in his pants or he breaks and tears her clothes off before he fucks her.

Either way, I'm here for it.

Eden grinds back on my dick like it's her favorite toy.

"You want my fingers inside you, sweet thing, or my dick?" I lick my way along her neck, leaving tiny bites that I soothe with soft sucks and kisses afterward. She moans and writhes and clamps down on my fingers. I'm barely inside her, just to the first knuckle, enough to tease all fuck out of the girl in my arms. Enough to make her drench her shorts to uselessness.

Christ, I need her thighs locked around my head.

"You gonna be okay if I lick you for a while? Can you entertain Sawyer, make sure he doesn't leave, sweet thing?"

"I want you both inside me," she moans mindlessly, riding the tips of my fingers though it's nowhere near enough to get her off.

But her words will do it.

"You want Sawyer, lovely?" I kiss the corner of her mouth, sliding my tongue in when she parts her lips.

She mumbles a reply around my tongue, kissing me back as she twists in my hold, still riding my hand.

"What was that, sweet thing?" I pull back, letting her roll beneath me.

Eden holds out a hand, but not to me.

Sawyer's sharp inhale is audible in the stillness. Then he's beside us, his mouth on hers as I rear over them both.

"Enjoy that sassy as fuck mouth," I mutter, wiggling my hand inside her shorts. She cries out as I begin to pull her clothing down, lifting her hips to help me. Her hands are already busy tugging at Sawyer's shirt. That disappears, along with her own clothes and suddenly Eden is naked beneath us, hot and wet and dripping and perfect.

"Mother of god," Sawyer rasps reverently, his mouth inches from hers. He glances down at me. "On your back, sunshine."

I grin, flipping to my back and haul Eden's legs to either side of my face. She shrieks when my tongue touches her from underneath, air kissing her clit, but her body won't be bare for long.

"What—"

"Relax, firefly," Sawyer tells her above me, his voice muffled as her legs close around my ears.

I lick and suck at her pussy, her hole weeping all over my chin. Juices dribble across my collar bone. A boot connects with my shin and I grunt, knowing it's just Sawyer getting himself naked. A rough hand grips my cock through my jeans and I whimper, closing my eyes as I taste her and let him work me roughly at the same time. I can't come like this, spread out beneath them both, but what he does in a moment I know might kill me.

My jeans are stripped off, and then Sawyer's hand is on my bare cock, stroking me sweetly.

"Cody likes it when I play with him but won't let him come," Sawyer explains my kinks to Eden as I lick her. Embarrassment fuels my arousal. I groan as my cock stiffens in his hand.

She gushes for me as he toys with her. His fingers slide into her cunt along with my tongue, feeding me her cream. She moans, the sound a vibration that travels along her entire body. Every taste is heaven, and every touch of his is torture. I lap her up, straining to wiggle my tongue close to her clit to give her relief.

"He's going to lie there and lick us both while I fuck you hard, gorgeous. Then he's going to clean you. And, only if you let him, can he fuck you later. If you say no, then he won't get to come at all tonight. But he'll make you orgasm as many times as you need. Won't you, Fox?"

I mumble my reply as his balls press to my mouth, his cock grinding her cunt and clit.

Eden cries out at the much needed contact that I can't provide from my position. I suck on Sawyer's balls, laving them in a bath, nice and wet.

Sawyer groans, rubbing his sac in my face as he grinds on Eden. "Fuck firefly, you feel good. Gonna fill you up now, breed you so you're full."

She moans, her heels digging into my ribs. My legs fall open, my dick ignored as I take a hold of Sawyer's cock and guide him into her dripping cunt.

He pauses at her entrance, and I lick them both,

getting them nice and sopping. Worshipping at the altar that was made for me. Sawyer ignores me, sliding into her until his balls rest against my lips. He stays there as I suck gently, rolling his sac in my mouth as he kisses her from their noises. I reach up, holding his ass cheeks so he's as deep inside her as he can go. When he starts to shift, I release my grip but hold him close.

And then he moves.

I groan, trying to keep up as he fucks my face and our girl together, dominating both of us. Her cries match her dripping hole. I lap frantically, winding my tongue between them. Her juices cover me. She gushes all over my neck and chest as they fuck, coming over and over again. I'll be covered in her scent forever at this rate. I'm not sure if it's from the extra stimulation I give or what Sawyer's doing, but she fucking loves it.

Sawyer doesn't last long, he's so turned on by our teasing. His orgasm is huge. He fills her, pounding deep, then pulls out to lodge his cock deep in my mouth, still pulsing his milky seed as their mixed liquids dribble onto my cheeks.

I moan, squeezing his ass cheeks rhythmically.

"Aww, toy. Suck me clean. Did you think I forgot you?" He rubs his cock in my mouth, fucking my throat gently.

Impossibly, he's hard again. I moan, sucking him clean until he's thick and full. He jams his cock into Eden's cunt again, flooding my face with their fluids as he runs against me, stimulating her. The moans she makes are the most precious, stunning sounds. Every cry wakes my cock up. I nearly disgrace myself, and reach for my dick, but he knocks my hand away.

"Don't you dare touch yourself," he growls. "Lick her."

I do as commanded as he rolls onto his back. Eden rides him, twisting impossibly to face me. I swipe the cum from my face, leaning in to suck her clit.

Her response is instantaneous. Short nails dig into my scalp as she grips my hair, and she rides his cock and my face all at once.

"Fuck," she screams, bearing down. Her pulses are so strong that I can feel them through her body and into his. Sawyer groans again, pushing his hips up as he comes a second time.

I stroke her gently, waking her clit up. "That was beautiful." I kiss her legs, cleaning the wet mess we've made of our girl. "My God, you're stunning."

"Cody." She launches into my arms, wrapping her hands about my neck. "Don't let go."

"Never. I'll hold you all night," I promise her,

knowing that what we've just done is well beyond anything she's likely ever experienced. "Lie between me and Sawyer?"

He watches her with heavy eyes, trailing his fingers along her thighs. "You gonna let Cody play with you, firefly, or are you gonna make him suffer? It's a game we like to play."

Usually just between us, but that's not how the statement comes out.

Eden looks back at me, her eyes wide.

I shrug, reaching for Sawyer's hand and close his firm grip around my cock, letting my hands fall away. "What can I say? I like to be—fuck," I mutter. "I like someone else to make a toy out of me. Use me." The humiliation of admitting my kink sends me spiraling higher into my state of arousal.

"That's so hot," Eden whispers.

"You like that, huh?" Sawyer tucks her into his chest as he works me over. "Are you gonna play with him, let him come in your pussy and feel pleasure, or are you gonna watch me edge the fuck out of our boy for the night?"

She shivers. "Play with him," she murmurs. "You first, then me?"

"Eden," I murmur, precum dribbling out of the top of my cock. Sawyer smears the bead away with his thumb.

He laughs as I stare into her face, already beyond desperate. "I love how you think, firefly." He kisses his cheek. "Spread your legs and play with your clit for me." I groan as his grip on my cock tightens. "If you come, Fox, you'll be licking my balls for the next month while I fuck her and you'll never see the inside of this perfect pussy. Is that clear?" Sawyer stares down at me. I nod. "Good. Now kiss her until she comes. When she does, you can slide your cock into her. Then you can clean her. And she'd better come again on your tongue."

"Thank you," I manage as he releases my cock and grips my neck, pushing me against her. His hand never leaves the back of my neck, massaging me as I kiss her. The need to grind against her is agonizing, but I try to keep my rhythm slow and not desperate.

Eden's moans are the stuff of fucking perfection as she works her clit. My eyes are closed but her body hums with tension as I slide my hands along her arms and cup her face, kissing her with the sort of need that conveys everything.

It doesn't take long. Seconds after Sawyer pushes me onto her she flexes in my arms. Her cry and the scent of her orgasm is fresh and salty. I push her legs wide before her cunt finishes fluttering and dive inside. His hand is still on the back of my neck as I burrow deep into her, fucking her hard and fast and rough.

Eden's cries wrap around us all. Sawyer's mouth is on her neck, his fingers teasing her nipples as I plow into her over and over. A moment before I thought I'd come too fast. Now I feel like I'll never come in time.

Her pussy pulses with an endless series of orgasms as she rides me over and over. Her mouth breaks from mine, her head tipping back. A sharp cry leaves her lips and then—

A darkness fades the world around the edges of my vision as her pussy contracts so tight on my cock that I can't breathe. Sawyer swears, his arms wrapping around us both, catching us as we tumble. I'm still fucking her, but I have no control. Eden's scream is the last thing I hear as I black out. Zero breath is left in my lungs, the pressure gripping my cock too great.

And when I come, it's painful enough that my scream matches hers.

Then we all fall together.

CHAPTER SEVEN

EDEN

"The fuck happened?"

"I thought she'd ripped my dick off."

"You passed out."

"Best mother fucking orgasm of my life."

"I'd do it all over again."

"You're not the only one who came."

The voices I recognize are distant, but not too far away. My brain refuses to make sense of anything as I surface from the deep void my mind retreated to after the hell I experienced.

Not the sex with Cody and Sawyer—that may have been the best thing I've ever done in my life.

No, the hell was the fact that in the middle of Sawyer and Cody fucking me, I reached an arm over my head and grabbed a leg not attached to my other lovers.

Well, in a way, it was.

That leg was denim covered and attached to Beau Hansen.

He's followed us out here.

Why we thought we could get away with anything without him knowing, I have no idea. Beau Hansen sees *everything*. I should know. He followed me to NYC twice, though I don't think the other Winterfox boys know. He stalked me a few times in college—but no one else is aware of that either. He knows about my parents.

And he still pushed me away back at the house.

But he turned up an hour—a few hours maybe, ago?—and he stood there, watching as Cody screwed me back into Sawyer's body. He watched the three of us wrap ourselves around each other.

Beau stood there, watching, and held my gaze as I came harder than I've ever come in my life.

"It wasn't your fault." Sawyer and Cody talk quietly above me.

I'm still tangled between them, but Cody looks cleaner when I surface, cracking first one eye then the other.

"What's not his fault?" I yawn widely. It's still

dark above us. The light hasn't changed, or maybe it has. "What time is it?"

"Three fifty a.m.," Sawyer says without looking.

"You're cleaner," I tell Cody.

"The river's icy. Good for a dip," he says impishly, leaning in for a kiss.

I let him explore my mouth, lifting me into his arms until I straddle him. My body is bare. I shiver until Sawyer slides in behind us.

"Let her sleep," he murmurs. "We're gonna wear her out."

"I'm awake," I protest. "And you're here."

"See? She's awake," Cody mutters against my mouth. "And she tastes damn fine."

I lean back against Sawyer. "Wait, was Beau here?"

They both freeze.

"What do you remember?" Sawyer says finally, dislodging my attempt to kiss him.

I frown. "Reaching back, touching—someone. Seeing his face. There's only one man who can glare like that, let's be fair. And then..." I stop talking, though my face heats.

Cody nudges me, trailing his hands across my breasts. "And then?" he teases, his easy nature resurfacing as he circles my nipples.

Sensation slams me fresh. "Stop that." I bat at

his hands, but he refuses to be deterred. Soft touches twirl around my breasts. I breathe shallowly, knowing I'm already dripping between them. "You're impossible," I whisper, rolling my hips.

"Fuck, that's pretty." Sawyer watches me through hooded eyes. "Tell us, firefly."

"I— He was here. Beau. We watched each other while you... While we all fucked. And then I came."

"Mmm," says Cody, thickening beneath me.

"More," Sawyer encourages me, adding his fingers to the pair already teasing my breasts, stroking my nipples sweetly. "Details matter, Eden."

"He was here. And I came. I came so hard that I don't remember what came nexxxtttt," I cry out, heat gushing between my legs.

Sawyer's large hand is there, cupping my sex to catch the fluid, smearing it all over me. "Fuck, that's a beautiful mess. Look at that." He holds up a glistening hand. "If Beau wants you, firefly, and he can make you come like that but he doesn't want to stay around, that's his problem." His hand grips the back of Cody's head. "Lick,' he says idly, pushing the other man down between my legs.

Cody's head disappears. A moment later his tongue touches the tender skin on my thighs. I moan, clapping my hands over my mouth.

"Oh, fuck," I pant event though he's not licking

anything important. I've just come and I'm still so turned on. How is that even possible?

Cody's tongue creeps closer to my cunt, the tiniest flicks leaving me on edge. I whimper out the moment his mouth is on me, sucking and soothing in gentle strokes while Sawyer kisses my mouth, stealing my sounds away for himself. Neither are enough to make me come on their own, but together? I shudder and shake in their arms, liquid and trembling as Cody slides his body against mine, flooding his mouth then his hand as they bring me to the edge again and again.

"Wow," I whisper, my vision dulling. I lie between them. "Maybe I do need that nap after all."

"We'll look after you, sweet thing." Cody kisses me, letting me taste myself on his lips. I moan, winding my hands through Cody's hair and arch my back, wondering if Beau is around, if he's watching.

Some part of me hopes we're alone, that it's just us.

Another part of me hopes he's there, where I can't see him, and that seeing us together hurts like hell.

THE BOYS ARE out when I wake next, the air turned cold, though the light is different. The sun hasn't risen yet. I guess it's about an hour before dawn, that strange time when the air is still, nothing is quite awake yet and the world is quiet.

It's my favorite time of day, though in NYC there was little time to appreciate it. Out here, that's a different story.

I slip from between Sawyer and Cody's warm bodies, grab a dampish towel that Cody must have used during the night after his impromptu bath, and pad barefoot and naked toward the river. Mentally, I know the river will be frigid. This far north, the water is *always* cold. No amount of summers here can remind me of that.

The first toe in the water draws a stifled yelp from me. Biting the bullet, I slide from my mossy rock and submerge beneath a small waterfall. My body cramps, telling me what a stupid idea jumping in was. I flail beneath the waterline, aiming for up and hit the bedrock instead.

Stupid, stupid.

In the pre-dawn light I can't even tell which way is up. *Really fucking stupid, Eden.* I reverse my trajectory and push my toes hard against the only surface I can find and pray I head in the right direction. My head breaches the surface a moment later. Chill morning air sucks into my lungs.

I clamber back onto my mossy rock, wet, but alive. Shivers take hold of me as I wrap my arms around my legs. Okay, so jumping in the river was stupid. Death defying even, but at least I'm clean and awake.

The damp towel I brought with me and left up the bank drops over my head. I grapple with it like a ghost under a sheet.

"Cute," I mutter at the boys' trick. "Just because you can jump in and not drown doesn't mean you should sneak up on people."

"It wasn't your finest moment." The deep voice that greets me belongs to neither Cody nor Sawyer, and is far too close for any sort of comfort, especially if he just watched me emerge from the water naked.

And dive in. Or nearly die because I mistook the bottom of the river for the surface.

Damnit, he saw that too. Just like he watched us last night.

"And you so chivalrously dived in to help," I snark back at Beau, not bothering to turn to face my night stalker.

Mostly because my face is burning with a fresh wave of humiliation. I don't think it's anything close to the sort that Cody enjoyed last night.

"If you hadn't found your way up I might have fished you out. Or maybe the others would have found you. They seem to be so attached to you now." Beau's voice grows distant though I don't think he's moved.

"Gee, thanks." Considering he stalked me for my first two years of college, I thought maybe he'd care more. But perhaps I misinterpreted all those late night trips to my apartment. The phone calls, the neediness. "I'm just one more person out of your life, huh?"

"Is that what you think?"

I huff and huddle within the confines of my wet, borrowed towel. "How else would you like me to interpret your midnight visits, Beau? I asked you to stay in New York. I came to your door, and you pushed me away. And last night..." I turn to face him in full and find him leaning against a tree a few yards away.

Those dark blue eyes stare back at me, impenetrable as always.

I forge ahead, glaring back at him. "You were there, watching us. *I touched you*. And you didn't do anything. You just...watched us," I finish somewhat lamely.

His eyebrows rise. "Is that not a kink I can share with Sawyer?"

I swallow hard. "How long were you there?"

"Long enough."

Fuck.

Beau waits a beat longer, then turns away.

"Wait!"

He pauses.

Why am I chasing him? Why do I care? He obviously doesn't. But I...do.

Both Cody and Sawyer gave me the gift of truth last night. Several times, both theirs and mine. Now it's time to pay that gift forward.

"I came back because I can't go home." I swallow hard at the admission that threatens to floor me even though the mossy ground that covers my rock can't get much more solid.

"You have a house." Beau's voice is sharp, his words abrupt. "You don't need to invade mine."

"It's empty, Beau. They're gone. I buried them a year ago. A year that I haven't seen you, or anyone. A year since the calls stopped. Since I spoke to..." Desperation fills my heart as I trail off because I'm repeating myself. The tears that always slam me when I bring this up cloud my vision. I force them back into their hiding place, willing them to stay away. He won't want to see them and right now neither do I. It's self pity, that's all, and right now it's selfish. Beau has lost just as much as me. "A year of silence that I broke in coming here." *To find you.*

"To fuck my friends. I heard that little conversation about no underwear, Miss Jane. Your point in coming here, for either me or them, is clear."

"I'm so glad you know everything, Hansen," I shoot back, standing. The towel unravels from my body, drifting to my feet in a wet slap to the rock. The action leaves me bare to the air's cold kiss and his gaze as the sky lightens a fraction. The night is still that purplish haze but it's enough. He can see plenty. "This? Is this what you're talking about, Hansen? Because this? My bag, my clothes? The 'no underwear' issue? That's everything I have. I paid my college fees. I paid for my accommodation. I fed myself, I got evicted," —I tick off each item on my fingers. My hip pops out and I don't give a single flying fuck of how childish I look or how I sound sassing back to him. Beau Hansen needs to know exactly how this came about— "I closed off mom and dad's debts. I spent a full month on the fucking streets in New York while I took my exams and graduated, grimy as all fuck under my grad gown. I bartered my last art piece instead of selling it so I could afford the bus trip back here, and I arrived at your doorstep. The clothes I wore? I saved those so you would never know. I was *never* going to tell you.

And I never wanted to show you the state of the underwear I wore. I showered once at a truck stop with money that I earned from drawing portraits of passengers. I got enough for meals on the way here. In fact if you check my bag, I have a dollar and sixty-five cents to my name. That's it. That's all I have. And that godforsaken house that I can't get rid of that my parents left me after they drank themselves stupid and slammed their pitiful lives into a tree. At least your father—"

"Eden," Beau warns me.

"At least your father," I pant, exhausted after the monologue of my life that's been building inside me since their deaths. I step closer to him. "At least your dad had kindness and dignity and– and—" I can't stop the tears that course down my face as I shut down completely.

Beau grips my arms fiercely. "My father hated me. He disowned me before he died, took my name off this land and told me that I have no place in the world. I have nothing more than you, Eden Jane, and I live here by the grace of the two men who fucked you into submission last night while I watched. The girl I used to love." His chest heaves as my heart shatters fresh.

"Used to?" I whisper, my words barely a sound, less than a breath.

Beau stares down at me a heartbeat longer. A sigh slips from him, the tension melting off his bones as he folds his arms around me, winding me tight into his chest. "Fuck, Eden. Seeing you with them last night— A part of me died," he rasps into my hair.

My tears destroy the front of his shirt. "I wish you'd have—"

His fingers dig into my hair, my scalp, pulling my head back. "Say it," he hisses into the fading darkness.

"I wish it had been you."

"Better."

"Too."

"*Eden.*" My name is like a promise and a curse rolling from his lips. "Get on your knees." His hands press to my shoulders.

My legs give without resistance. I know this game. It's one we've played many times. It's his favorite.

But it's mine, too.

And we only play it when he's giving me what I want.

I sink to the mossy carpeted forest floor with my feet tucked beneath my knees and bat my eyelashes. "Like this?"

Beau catches my chin, squeezing firmly as he

works his belt free. "Breathe slowly, Eden," he murmurs.

I let my eyes close as the head of his cock nudges my lips. There's no thought of resistance as he pushes inside my mouth, no chance that my hands will rise from my knees to rake at his denim covered thighs.

How easily we return to old habits.

Beau's cock bumps the back of my throat. I swallow gently against the intrusion, getting used to him as he leans over me, shifting his weight. My tongue slides under his cock, swirling and teasing as he groans softly. He'll keep this between just us for as long as possible, because he's possessive and jealous like that, but he won't be able to keep it that way forever.

Beau Hansen isn't the only possessive asshole out there. After last night, the feeling of Cody and Sawyer's hands on me, their need wrapped around me, teasing and freaking *caring* how they spent their hours and with me... It's greedy as fuck but I want all three of them, too.

Right now though, I just want one man.

Beau strokes my cheek in a featherlight touch. "Easy, Eden. I want to see you struggle for me. Give me your tears."

Oh, fuck. It's one of *those* nights.

I mumble my protest around his cock stuffed in my mouth, and he laughs softly.

"That's cute, love. Now swallow for me." Beau pushes forward, his hand clasped around the back of my head, holding me in place.

I choke.

Heat rushes through me, coating my thighs with need, at my lack of control. Drool drips from the corners of my mouth at the fullness he provides. I swallow quickly, trying to keep up as Beau pushes me deeper, merciless. I raise my eyes to meet his, but he only stares down at me, arched lips curved upwards in the faintest smile.

A pulse begins between my legs and I gasp.

Just as fast he withdraws, leaving me coughing and choking on air.

"Asshole," I whisper. "I was about to—"

"I know," he cuts me off. "You'll come when I say and not a moment before. Clear?"

"Fuck you," I mutter, swiping my hand across my mouth.

Beau's fingers lace in my hair, tugging my head back sharply. "Breathe."

I suck in a deep breath before his cock fills my throat again, cutting off my air.

And repeat.

Beau edges me to the point of insanity, stealing

my air, giving me the hope of pleasure only to rip it away. I'm a whimpering, crying mess by the time the sun rises, and I realize we have an audience.

"She's pretty on her knees." Sawyer watches me with his arms folded.

Cody sits on the ground, his hands looped around his knees. "You gotta let her come. She's fucking weeping for you, man. Tears and pussy."

I sob around Beau's cock that thickens impossibly, cutting off any chance of a breath. His hips flex, driving his length deeper into my throat. Their observations drive us higher. I gag, but it's on nothing as he fucks my throat. Pressure builds between my thighs and my hands clench.

"Fuck, she's good. Look at how well trained you are." Cody scoots closer, almost close enough to touch. I stretch a hand out, needing his support, but Beau bats it away.

I'm alone in this until he says otherwise.

Sawyer watching me is intense, his gaze a physical experience that touches every part of me until I overheat, writhing on the spot. I try to beg around Beau's cock but hardly any sound comes out as he jacks his hips, sending me reeling backwards. His hands keep me in place, pressed to his torso.

For the first time my palms leave my knees. I reach for him, needing to grasp for balance, but catch myself halfway. I fist my fingers into knots and raise them behind my head.

Beau's smile when I raise my gaze to meet his, is complete and utter victory. He grips my wrists at my nape and fucks me backward until my spine hits a tree.

Then his hips don't stop. I suck in breaths when he lets me have them and pray I can hold in between times, coughing and sobbing around his cock. And the whole time, my thighs are coated with my need, while I writhe against his body.

"Fuck," he growls finally, with drawing from my throat. "Stand up, Eden. Let them see you."

I stare up at him, gasping out huge breaths. Stand? Is he fucking serious? My legs will be lucky if they work at all after that. His laugh is echoed by Sawyer's while Cody offers me a commiserating look.

Beau's hands under my armpits hoist me upright. My legs support me, just, as he presses me back against the tree that just supported me.

"Pretty, messy thing," he mocks me, pulling off his shirt. "Clean yourself up."

"No." Sawyer stalks forward, ripping Beau's shirt out of his hands and tossing it aside. "I wanna see her all fucked and fucked up. She's sweetest this way." He strokes my hair back from my face.

I whimper as his thumb presses over my swollen lips.

Beau smirks. "Is this how you're prettiest for us?" he murmurs, catching my jaw in his hand. "Open your mouth, Eden."

I don't fight, just nod, letting my lips part.

Beau tips my head back, arching over me. A thin line of drool dribbles from his lips into my mouth. "Swallow."

"Not yet." Sawyer leans in, his mouth hovering so close to my open lips and spits into my mouth. He taps my legs apart. "Now swallow, firefly. You're ours."

I swallow, staring at the wide eyed, and cry out as a tongue laps at the mess between my thighs. "Cody!"

He doesn't answer, his tongue too busy on my pussy.

Beau strokes Cody's hair back. "Get her nice and ready. We do this together." He looks at Sawyer, who nods.

I let them lift my legs and drape them over Cody's broad shoulders so the other mountain rancher takes my weight. It feels insane to let him hold me like this but when he sucks my clit and rolls the bundle of nerves with his tongue, I scream my orgasm into Beau's waiting mouth.

His tongue sweeps across mine with the authority of a man who knows everything I want and is prepared to give me exactly that. I let go of reality as Beau kisses me, knowing I'm gushing all over Cody and riding his face. The man below me groans, and the rancher kissing me lets out a laugh.

"Christ, Eden. You'll drown him. All that from a kiss?" Beau stares down at me, as though willing me to defy him.

I stare back, my sass locked into place. "All that because I missed you."

He groans, slamming his mouth to mine. Cody shifts, and then Beau's between my legs, pushing deep. I scream my pleasure into his shoulder as he thrusts hard. The sense of fullness burns, but in the best of ways. I'm soaked, thanks to his edging and Cody's talented mouth. It doesn't take much for Beau to bottom out inside me even with his cock rock hard. He lifts my legs around his hips, dropping me lower onto him.

"Oh, fuck. Too much, too much," I chant, uncaring that my back rubs against the tree's rough bark.

"Not yet, firefly." Thick fingers trace sweet patterns across my collarbone. "Tell me when you're at breaking point. Maybe then we'll consider stopping." Sawyer sucks on my neck, marking me as I gush all over Beau's cock. "Or maybe we won't."

Beau swears, fucking me faster until Sawyer's hands slam onto my hips, stilling us both. The blunt head of his cock nudges at the entrance to my pussy. I squeak as I work out what he's doing, wiggling my hips. Beau's already there, filling me and Sawyer's so thick—there's no way they'll both fit. If they're both inside me...

I'll break for them.

Sawyer's hand closes on my throat, squeezing rhythmically until I gush for him. Beau's given him my weakness, and he weaponizes it now. I moan and tip my head back, barely sucking in a breath long enough when Sawyer's mouth slams over mine. I glide my tongue along his, working my hips in time with Beau's.

"No chance," I pant. "You won't fit."

Sawyer smiles, tucking our bodies together. "Oh, firefly. Why don't you bite down on Beau for me?" He thrusts forward, and I scream.

I think I scream. My world whites out, and I'm locked in place between them. I can't move, the pleasure of him inside me is so great. I'm pulsing and screaming and—

Fluid slicks my thighs in a deluge as I writhe for them, clamping down as they both groan with me.

"Christ, I've never seen her come like that before." Beau kisses me gently. "Love. Tell me you're okay?" His mouth is soft on mine. Tender. Sweet.

I nod tiredly. My legs wind like jelly around his waist. "Can you put me down now?

"Not a chance, firefly." Sawyer shifts behind me. A heaviness inside me moves with him.

"Oh, fuck." I dig my nails into Beau's back. "This is impossible."

"You came hard enough to make us both lose hold of our sanity, love. Trust me, you're okay. We'll make this good for you."

I shiver in Beau's arms, tucking my face into his shoulder as my pussy clenches tight on both of them. "Like that?" I ask sweetly.

"Yeah. Fuck, that's good, Eden." Beau shifts. "Ready?"

"Not really," I admit.

"When you are, brother," Sawyer speaks over me.

"Huh?" I push up to look between them.

"Good. I need to ruin her."

What the fuck?

Beau and Sawyer move at the same time. The sensations that ram through me don't seem possible as they move in sync like one person. Both slide in together all the way, then all the way out.

It's like they're fucking me with one single, giant cock.

I close my eyes, biting down on Beau's collar bone, but he doesn't seem to notice. We're all so far gone with Cody between us, lapping at every inch of soft skin he can find to play with.

I shudder and scream as the boys fill my pussy over and over, stretching and working me as we find me ways to torture each other. Them, working together. Me? Squeezing their cocks with my cunt as hard as I can, ignoring them, petting Cody as often as I can reach him.

Finally, Sawyer pulls out with an oath, milking ropes of warm cum across my back. The fluids don't have a chance to cool as Cody's there, rubbing his hands through the mess.

"Have you tried anything else, sweet thing?" he murmurs as Beau fucks me slowly, his rhythm steady and maddening.

I gasp for each breath, barely listening to him. "I mean, I have some toys. And I've played around with some— some plugs, and tails and things." The admission heats my cheeks.

"Perfect." Cody scoops up Sawyer's cum and strokes it along my crack. "Are you okay if I play here, Eden?" He rubs his fingertip over my asshole, pushing in a little.

The tight muscle gives with his insistent touch. I moan as his finger slides into me to the first knuckle then the second as Beau keeps his pace steady. Cody works his finger in and out, then adds a second. The burn isn't as bad as I expect, and I'm gaping and leaning into Beau, clinging to him as Cody works me over.

Beau never lets up, claiming my mouth in a series of kisses that are the addictive sort. I let out a sob and his arms fold around me. "Shh, love. I'll hold you after. Let me give you—" I shudder, bearing down on his cock and Cody's presses to my asshole. "Fuck, there you go." Beau looks down at me tenderly. "You're perfect."

My cream coats all of us.

"Perfect," Cody echoes. "Keep fucking her, Beau. She's so beautiful when we're using her." His cock, coated with Sawyer's cum, slides into my ass.

The feeling of both of them inside me is so different to Beau and Sawyer. I moan out my need, rocking between them. Every part of me tingles, over sensitized, ready to scream for them again.

I squeeze Cody hard for the compliment and he lets out a long moan. "Thank you," I murmur, the picture of innocence for him while he fucks my ass.

"Perfect," he whispers again, sliding into me

balls deep as I gasp for air. "That's it, sweet thing. Struggle for all of us. Can you come?"

Beau slides his fingers between us, working my clit. "She'll come. Eden's gonna cream all over me and she's gonna clamp her asshole on your cock until you pump her full. Aren't you a good girl for us?"

I squeeze his cock tight in my cunt. "Yes, Beau."

He grips my hips tight. "Good. Now, I promised to ruin you."

"Ohhhh—" I let out an embarrassingly long moan as Beau slams into me, over and over. His pace is matched by Cody who rails my asshole, gaping me open. Beau's fingers never leave my clit, working me longer and faster until I explode for him too.

"Fill me," I beg them both, squeezing down as hard as I can. "Please?"

"Oh hell. She begs." Cody's voice makes it sound like all his Christmases have come at once.

"Wait til she's on her knees and you're behind her when she pleads for you. Best fucking feeling." Beau slams into me and lets out a shout. His seed fills me and trickles down my thighs. A second later Cody follows him, filling my other hole until I'm plugged and brimming.

I fall forward onto Beau's chest, Cody's momentum pushing me onto him. They're both buried hilt deep inside me, and I know I'll never be the same.

They proposed to ruin me, and I accept their punishment for leaving. But that treatment isn't without a little exchange of my own. I might be theirs but they're mine, too, even if just in this moment.

My senses return as breath sucks into my lungs. "You're gonna let me dive back into that freezing river soon, right?"

I pull Beau's mouth idly down to mine as Cody works himself free of my body, swearing softly. His fingers trace around the hole he's stretched, a groan leaving him.

Beau laughs against my mouth. "Love, I half want to watch you walk back to the homestead, dripping and struggling just so we can lay you out on the bathroom floor and fuck you again." He looks around the group.

Sawyer leans in, kissing my tender lips hard. "Sounds cute, firefly. But go clean yourself up, and let Cody carry you in so you don't drown this time, okay?"

I wince. Does everyone know about the river incident before dawn?

Cody lifts me off the ground. "One princess river treatment coming right up."

I squeal as he walks me into the water, letting the icy sensation soak up to our necks. "I didn't know you did princess treatments," I manage when I can speak again.

"For you?" Cody nudges my mouth with his in a gentle kiss. "Always, honey badger. You gonna let me lie you back on the bank later and eat you while the other two watch?"

I gape at him. "Aren't you worn out? How on earth do you keep going?"

He shrugs. "You're everything to me, Eden. You always have been. Sawyer, too, though he'll probably never say it. We've been in love with you at least as long as Beau has. He was just the first one to say it, make it formal."

I fall quiet for a moment, curled in his arms. The warmth of him soaks into me against the cold of the water. "I think I knew that, somehow the three of you were always there, looking after me. You were always around, and no one ever hurt me. I thought it was this place that I came back to. That it was Winterfox Woods that I fell in love with. But... It was you. All of you." I glance at the bank to find Beau and Sawyer watching us.

Cody wraps his arms tighter around me. "They can have you later, sweet thing. We'll share. But for right now, you're mine. And I intend to give the woman that I love every orgasm that she deserves."

I look up at him, my heart threatening to shatter fresh. "Are you being serious?"

Cody's easy smile has dropped away, but his warmth remains firmly in place. *Safe.* "I'll always love you, Eden. I always have. I just didn't know I could say anything without Beau whooping my butt. Back then, that seemed to matter."

I shrug, playing it cool though my heart leaps at his words. "I meant about the orgasms."

Cody's grin flies back to his face. "Sassy thing."

My shriek fills the clearing as he dunks me under the water, still holding onto me, then pulls me out onto the bank.

And as I lie there, shivering, with Beau and Sawyer pinning me down by a wrist and an ankle each, Cody does exactly what he promised.

He uses that talented tongue and presents me with as many orgasms as my body can handle until I'm begging for mercy from the mountain men of Winterfox Woods.

EPILOGUE

EDEN

Cutlery clatters around the Winterfox homestead formal dining table. The walnut behemoth is big enough to fill the giant space, which means we're all pushed far enough apart that talking is almost impossible. I feel like I can yell across the twenty-seater to the next man, or maybe roll my bread roll—*heh*—at Sawyer.

Beau sits at the head of the table alone, eating the roast that the boys put together in a rush after we finally made it back from the bunk house. I'm exhausted, and sore, and wearing clothes the years old that Beau kept from the last time I stayed with him.

Before.

And they're happy. Okay, so we're all happy.

A happy, happy family.

So why is the air so stilted in this stuffy, airless room?

Another knife clangs on a plate. That's the only sound in the closed room, apart from Cody's pointed cough as everyone else eats in silence. I sneak a glance at him, unsure if I should be horrified, or snicker. I'm pretty sure that last is what he's concealing. Come on. It's Cody. He takes *nothing* seriously.

After a few extra bites, Sawyer pushes his high backed chair away from the table.

"Is this what you wanted, Beau?" He addresses the head of the table.

"Mmm?" Beau pauses mid-bite and cocks his head.

Cody coughs. The room falls silent.

Sawyer's face reddens. "I said," he shouts. "Is this, *WHAT YOU WANTED?*"

Beau shrugs. "I heard you. I just wanted to see what you'd do."

Sawyer's roll shatters in his thick fingers. Cody snorts into his roast and gravy.

I poke a fork in Beau's direction since there's no chance in hell that I'll be able to actually reach him. "You know, that wasn't very nice."

He shrugs again. "I know."

Cody leans back in his chair, looking between us like an umpire at a sports match. "What are we doing here?" He pauses. "I mean, we eat here every night. We don't say shit, and now we've added Eden to the mix. Unless we're putting her on the table for dessert..." He eyes me speculatively, "Then I suggest we throw this piece of wood out and replace it with a billiards table."

Beau blinks. "It's a family heirloom."

"A family who disowned you." Sawyer doesn't have a problem beating about the bush. Exasperation laces his tone.

"Thanks for that reminder." Beau pushes up from his chair. The legs scrape on the hard wood, no doubt scarring the surface.

I wince at the house's scream, its singular protest to the rift forming between the boys. My fingers grip the edge of the table. I want to say something, grab at Beau, but my body is exhausted from our playtime in the bunkhouse once we arrived from the end of our overnight camping trip in the field near the river. Their aim was to wear me out. They succeeded. Now, I have nothing left to defend one of the men I love so much.

My heart aches for him as my mouth opens. The softest sound creaks from my sore throat, but it's not enough to halt Beau's exodus from the room.

"Stop."

I jump at the authority in Cody's tone. Even Sawyer looks at him in mild surprise.

"Would you like to add to the calamity unfolding before you?" Beau looks over at Cody, his voice eerily calm and polite. Nothing gives him away except for the pulse jumping in his neck.

"Stop being a righteous shit." Cody looks straight at Beau and doesn't back down.

I'd cheer, except that I have no energy left. So I sit this one out while Sawyer stares with his mouth half open, his crumbling dinner roll destroyed between his hands.

"I think you've taken on some of Eden's bratty energy, Cody. Since when did you grow a pair?" Beau scoffs.

"Stop it," I manage. Barely. My voice is less than a thread.

All the humor of a few moments before has evaporated, leaving the room little more than a tense tinder box ready to explode.

Sawyer glances my way. "Eden's right. This isn't getting us anywhere," he says in a quiet voice that's loud enough to be heard in the strained silence between the two men at the table.

I know I'm a brat. Beau knows that. He's never had a problem with my attitude before. Hell, it's not even why we broke up the first time. It *is* why he followed me to NYU. How we are together is an addiction neither of us can kick. Is it sweet? Never. Toxic? Hells, yes.

But to call me out on it like he just did, or aim that same derision at Cody when he doesn't deserve it? That's going too far.

I push up on legs that wobble. "*Stop it.*" I shove my voice as far as it'll go. My throat aches, and the two words crack.

Sawyer is around the table and at my side in a second. His arms scoop me up, hauling me against his chest. I bat at his arms, but he refuses to let me go as he hauls me onto his lap. "Shh, firefly. This is a problem that's been boiling between us for much longer than since you've been here." He strokes my hair back from my face tenderly.

I look up at him, grateful for the intervention and touch my throat.

"I'm sorry we hurt you." He presses a kiss to my temple.

"I loved every second," I rasp. It's gentler on my throat somehow than whispering.

"One day has to be a record."

"Fuck off, Beau." Sawyer's chest rumbles, so I know who pushes back.

I shove at his chest and wave a hand. "No."

"See? Even Eden doesn't want a piece of your attitude." Sawyer seems inordinately pleased with this outcome.

I shove at his chest a second time. "*NO.*" I wave at Beau again. Beckoning him. "Come here," I rasp.

Beau swallows, his hands gripping the back of his chair.

"What, afraid of this tiny thing?" Cody goads him.

"Have you seen her in full action?" Beau mutters under his breath.

Even Sawyer cracks a rare laugh. "Do what she says."

"Fuck you." He comes anyway, rounding the table in long strides to face me where I'm wrapped in Sawyer's arms. "I'm here."

I gaze up at Beau, and hold out my hands. He stares back woodenly. Everything he said back in the forest slams into me, and suddenly I understand in full color what's happening here. And... I think I know how to fix it. Maybe. Or maybe what I'll do next will shatter their already fragile bond further apart than ever. It's a risk I'll take because Beau's about to walk. I can see that in his face, in his wide stance when he doesn't reach for me.

And it's not because I'm wrapped up in his best friend's arms. If they're even still best friends right now. But that bond *is* still between them. Deep down. It's always been there. These men grew up together. They've been through tragedy, emotional pain. Personal loss.

Abandonment.

I press deeper into Sawyer's embrace, and let Beau see that. "I know you're hurting. I know that. I feel it," I whisper, my voice the thinnest thread. "You were there for me when I needed you, but also you weren't. Now I need you to fix something for me."

His hands fist at his sides. "I'll do anything for you. You have to know that."

I do. I'm counting on that. "I know. Kneel."

Beau drops to his knees before me without a word.

My eyes close for the briefest second, my heart breaking for him. "Not for me." My eyes open. "For them."

Pain and panic is etched across his face in deep lines. "Eden–"

"Do what she says." Cody's voice is harsh as he backs me. "Crawl, Beau. To me."

I hold my breath. Beau was on the verge of

walking away a moment before. Either I've broken something to the point of irreparable with this crazy, insane thought, or—

"Eden," Beau murmurs, his face drawn and distraught.

"Please?" I hold out my hand, the tips of my fingers shaking with exhaustion.

Sawyer's arms tighten.

Then warmth brushes my fingers, the most delicate admission, before I see something I never thought would actually happen.

Beau Hansen crawls across the floor to where Cody kicks his chair out, his legs spread wide apart to make space. When he gets there, Cody's hand rests on his head. He leans down and whispers something into Beau's ear. I don't get to hear what he says, but Beau's shoulders shake. Then his whole body. Cody's arm wraps around the back of Beau's neck and he presses the other man's cheek to his inner thigh.

I hold my breath, expecting resistance, but Beau lets Cody guide him into the submissive pose. Cody stokes his cheek, murmuring things I still can't hear, but his gaze softens as he looks down at his oldest friend with forgiveness in his eyes.

After a moment, Cody taps Beau's cheek and directs him back to us.

Sawyer's grip on my turns to steel. I try to shift sideways on his lap to give him space, but he refuses to let me budge.

"I'm not your shield," I murmur, unwilling to become a barrier between the two men who need to make this right between them.

Beau kneels before us, his hands on his knees, eyes on me.

"Firefly?" Sawyer's voice is ragged in my ear. "This is your show."

I shake my head, but even Beau looks to me for guidance. *Okay, maybe it is.* For some reason, Cody is better at this than Sawyer, which blows me away. I'm proud of the younger man, but now I have this clusterfuck to mediate.

"The two of you have been at odds for a long time. Sawyer?" The arms around me tense to snapping point. *Me.* I'm the thing that will snap if Sawyer grips me any harder. "Gentle," I murmur, wondering if I'm talking about his intended words, or me.

"I was an asshole to you." It's Beau who starts.

I stare at him in shock, unsure if he's talking to me, Sawyer or both of us.

"I pushed you away and never let you explain why. I begged you to stay and refused to let you be you." His gaze flits back and forth between us.

Okay, so it looks like it's both of us at once. That wasn't my plan, but if it works...

"I tried to help you after your dad disinherited you," Sawyer grates out, like the words are the world's hardest admission but have been on his tongue, waiting to come out for an age. "I gifted you my half of the ranch, for fuck's sake. It's still in your name, Beau. I never changed that."

Beau's face hardens as he stares at the man behind me.

And... we're back at an impasse.

If a rancher's ego falls in Winterfox Woods and no one there to hear it, did it ever actually happen?

"Christ. I didn't know that," Cody breathes through the permeating silence that cloys the air in a sickening sense of ego and charity.

"I don't want your pity," Beau snarls. Or at least he tries to, but his words come out soft and broken instead. "I wanted a father who loved me and a mother who stayed instead of running off with your dad."

I blink. Welp. There are some family secrets about Winterfox Woods that have stayed under the proverbial carpet.

Cody blows out a breath. "I did know that," he admits.

Sawyer's hands flex on my arms. "We're both hurting. It's not your fault that our parents weren't who we thought any more. What you can do is fix who you've been to us for the past years. Be better, Beau. Be *here.* She needs you." He swallows and his hold on me gentles as he pushes me forward. "I need you."

I slide off Sawyer's lap, to the floor, away from Beau. This isn't my time.

It's theirs.

Sawyer leans his elbows on his knees until his face is level with Beau's. "I've needed you for so goddam long. I've cleaned this place up. I've cooked and served you dinner. I've watched you try to be the father for this place that you thought you needed to be, a replacement for what we all lost. The one man fucking show, but you know what? We don't need that. We never did. Because we are stronger *together.* And when you man up and realize that, you'll figure out that you can just be...you. With us." Sawyer reaches out and circles Beau's throat with his hand, pulling him closer. His hand closes, restricting his air.

I swear my heart stops in my chest. I look at Cody, trusting that he'll prevent the madness unfolding before us, but he holds out a hand instead. I grip the offering fiercely, needing his support. Giving him my trust.

"Anything," Beau forces out past Sawyer's grip, pushing hard to make his words clear and heard. "Just make it fucking work."

Sawyer squeezes his throat for a moment longer then nods, pulling Beau in for a hard kiss before he releases him. "Alright."

I blink, stunned. "That's it?"

Cody tucks me against his legs, one arm looped loosely across my chest. "Not quite, sweet thing." He crooks a finger in Beau's direction. "You're not done yet."

Beau crawls again, but this time the look on his face is determined, like a flame relit from within.

I skitter backward, my energy renewed, but there's nowhere to go. Cody's hold is loose, but he's not letting me out, and Sawyer watches me with his lips curled up in amusement.

"Wait," I whisper. "What—"

Beau's hands frame my head on either side as they clamp onto Cody's shins in a cage of sweat and sin. "You've been a thorn in my side for years, feral little creature," he growls. His lips are the barest inch from mine as he stares into my eyes.

I whimper, pressing backward into Cody's

warmth. The facade of safety surrounds me while the predator stares into my eyes. His arm tightened across my chest.

"Beau–" I breathe. "I'm—"

His knees tap mine apart, making space for his larger body on the floor between the other two men watching us. "Fuck, I love you, Eden." His mouth smashes down on mine in a possessive kiss that leaves me seeing the sorts of stars that fill the sky on a clear summer night above Winterfox Woods.

Beau steals a fraction of my sanity and my breath along with my heart. I pant as he pulls back a fraction, raising his eyes to meet Cody's. "I love you, you bratty little fucker," he growls, then looks over his shoulder. "And you too, you big grump."

"Yeah, you're a real sweetheart." Sawyer kicks at Beau's feet, jostling us.

Beau pushes my legs wider, sliding his hands along the insides of my thighs. I moan, already turned on at the thought of having him while the others watch us—*again*.

"We can't. I'm too sore," I protest.

The smile Beau offers is filled with the promise of sin that will take me through another sleepless night. He slithers down my body, taking my clothing with him. "But I'm not done groveling yet, love."

I close my eyes and let Cody hold me as Beau reminds me why I brat out for him and just how well he's capable of taming me...

With a little help from the men who love him almost as much as I do.

BONUS EPILOGUE

EDEN

The dip in the icy river at Winterfox was so worth it. Not just to be clean but..okay, yeah. It was to be clean. Cody walks alongside me through the dappled light beneath the heavy foliage we passed under to reach the clearing the night before.

One night, and everything has changed.

His fingers interlace through mine and he tugs me into his side. "Penny for your thoughts, honey badger," he murmurs.

Even Cody's effervescent spirit is muted this morning. Sawyer strides ahead of us, his steps sure but shorter than usual. Beau walks quietly behind us, just close enough for me to know he's there; not near enough to touch.

The tension between us builds with every step until I feel like I'm at breaking point and ready to snap.

Only, I'm not sure why.

"Hmm?" I twist to look up at Cody and find myself lost in his aquamarine eyes. "Everything is new. You. Us. Being with Beau again," I confess in a low voice that I pretend doesn't carry to the others flanking our steps.

Cody's hand squeezes mine. "Change is good, sweet thing. Adjusting is harder. It's accommodating the needs of others that's scary. Once you realize that the world is made up of more shapes than you and those you love, it's okay." He shrugs.

I shift closer to him. "Since when did you get so wise?" I remember a kid who used to ride the biggest bull he should never have been on, showing off every time I was around, or taking me out to try some new brew of moonshine he'd cooked up while ever Beau was too busy on the ranch to notice my absence until later.

Either way, it got him into a lot of trouble. *Wise* and *responsible* weren't words I ever equated with Cody Fox.

He shrugs. "I guess I grew up while you weren't

looking, sweet thing." His thumb sweeps across the back of my hand in a circular motion.

My heart beat ratchets up as Sawyer steps out of the trees, and we follow. Suddenly, the bunkhouse is in sight, and the fairytale is over.

Everything is real now.

I pull my hand from Cody's. "I guess this is me." I wrap my arms around myself, heading for the door in long steps. My slowest-fast retreat ever. "You boys have fun, huh? I'll just be here, you know... Give me a few jobs to earn my keep." I back toward the door as they turn to face me all in sync.

It's unnerving as fuck.

Beau rocks back on his heels, the faintest smile on his lips. He watches Sawyer prowl forward like he's gonna sit back and see how this one plays out.

I already know.

I twist and dart toward the door to my sanctuary, the key I pilfered from Sawyer's pocket in my hand. The silver of silver metal is in the lock, the handle turning beneath my hand before I take my next breath.

I'm safe. It's okay.

Not that I'm not safe with the boys, but I need space. I need to think. I need—

The arm that wraps around my waist is as thick as a tree trunk. It is neither safe nor space giving, and I have absolutely zero time to think as Sawyer hoists me off my feet. A yelp rips from my lips, my protest loud enough to echo off the spruces surrounding the bunkhouse.

The door to the bunk house opens under Cody's hand. He sketches a false bow before us, a playful smile on his lips. "My honey badger, your castle."

I hang upside down from Sawyer's unyielding arms and stick my tongue out at him.

Cody's eyes darken. "You'll need that later, sweet thing. I promise."

Breath escapes me as Sawyer crosses the threshold. His hand lands on my ass with a resounding crack, and suddenly I'm airborne. My squeak dies a short breath as I bounce on the sofa that's seen many better days before he cages me in. A hand lands on either side of my head, his knees framing my hips.

"Did you think you could just push us away now that the honeymoon is over, firefly?" Sawyer breathes, running his nose along my throat. "Fuck, she smells good." He goes from talking to me to *about* me and something in being objectified like that hits a switch on me.

Heat rushes through my body, leaving me tingling all over. My nipples pebble beneath my shirt as Beau and Cody crowd the head of the sofa, and wetness pools between my thighs.

"This." Beau reaches down to pinch a nipple, his fingers pincer tight. "This, Eden, shows just how much of a little fucking liar you re yo yourself. We know what you need." He rolls my nipple until I arch for him.

My mouth falls open, lashes shuttering on the vision of the three of them looming over me. It's a long held fantasy, one I've never admitted to anyone. Back then, I was Beau's girl, and I'd never cheat on him. But the thought of them all sharing me? That's one hell of a mountain man rush. Now? I writhe at the thought of them all touching me with his permission...*again*.

Sawyer pushes my legs wide with his knees. "Cody?"

A coldness touches my belly, hard and unyielding. My eyes fly open and I gasp at the sight of what looks like the world's biggest blade pressed against my skin. Sure, the flat of the blade, but it's still a motherfucking giant ass *knife*.

"Don't move, sweet thing," Cody murmurs, lifting the knife and licking the tip.

The tip that slices through denim like its tissue.

My shorts fall away as I pant, metal gliding over my bare pussy until my juices coat the blade.

"Fuck, you're ready for us, love," Beau murmurs, teasing my nipple as he leans down to lick my tongue, his kiss wet and open without sealing his lips to mine.

I moan at the depravity of it all. My thighs tremble against Sawyer's knees where he holds me open. His low growl is the only warning I need to remain still as Cody destroys my only other remaining piece of clothing—my shirt.

"That's all I own," I mewl as Sawyer takes the opportunity to spear his fingers, two of them, twisted and knuckle deep inside me.

I scream the rest of my protest as the boys laugh above me, breaking from Beau's depraved version of a kiss.

"Sweet thing, I think we'd have you here naked and in boots for the rest of your fucking life if it was our choice." Cody works his shirt off then his jeans as he talks, the boys making fast work of their own clothes as Sawyer fingers me. I can barely concentrate on Cody's voice over the pleasure slamming into me as I roll my hips to meet his touch. "We'll get you whatever you need, I promise. But today you're ours however we want."

"I—fuck, yes," I gasp as I cum on Sawyer's fingers, unsure what I just agreed to.

"Good girl." Beau pulls the tatters of my shirt

away and leans down to suck my nipple into his mouth. Cody does the same on my other side as Sawyer slides down, gliding his tongue over me.

I close my eyes, my mouth open in utter bliss. I can't breathe. I can't think.

I sure as hell can't form words when I'm begging and moaning and writhing beneath them all at once in a stimulation overflow of sensation.

"Fuck, you're drenching his face, love." Beau toys my nipple with his fingers as he finds my mouth with his in a sweet kiss. I moan against his lips, seeking his tongue, anything. He smiles. "Is that what you need, a thick cock in your mouth? My friend here needs your talents." He pats Cody's rump, urging the younger man to leave my breast alone.

Cody's cock presses to my lips. I open for him, swirling my tongue around his cockhead and sucking gently.

"She can take you," Beau murmurs. "Don't be so sweet with that tight throat. Choking makes her come faster than anything." He places Cody's hands on my face and urges his friend forward.

Cody's cock fills my throat. I glide my tongue beneath his length, attempting to swallow, but his rhythm is fast and the angle is wrong. I look up at Beau from the corner of my eye, reading his smirk and know this will be rough. I swallow gently, but end up gagging. Tears cloud my vision, and I'm done.

Cody bucks his hips and groans. "Fuck, she takes it deep."

"And she's cumming." Disbelief fills Sawyer's voice as I wrap my legs around his head, riding his face through the wave of pleasure.

"That's enough." Beau pulls Cody back, giving me air as our world grays a little at the edges. A second passes, then I cough, rolling to my side. My pussy still pulses around the fingers that Sawyer thrusts roughly inside me, keeping my orgasm going.

"Fuck, Beau," I whisper weakly. "I needed to keep that secret."

He strokes my hair. "Beautiful, I'm going to show them all your depravities tonight. We'll ruin you so that the only men you'll want are the three of us forever."

I whimper as he taps his cock to my lips, and take him deep to the back of my throat. Beau sets a hellish pace, knowing I can't keep up. Saliva coats my face, but he doesn't make me choke, not yet. It's like he's building up to something—

Sawyer's fingers scooping my cream from my

cunt and rubbing it across my asshole leaves me groaning.

"What if we never fuck your pussy for this session, firefly?" He squeezes my hip possessively. "What if we gape this little asshole and ruin your throat, leave you glistening and weeping and empty while you come over and over for us?"

I cry and come for him at the depravity of his words while Beau laughs above me. Cody strokes my hair and my face, wiping my tears away. I look to him for support but he just licks his fingers and blows me a kiss.

Then he's behind me, his cock lodged to my asshole as he jerks off, covering me in his mess.

"Perfect," Sawyer murmurs, sliding his fingers into my ass, stretching me.

I moan around the burn as Beau shoves his cock deeper. Suddenly I understand. This is what he was waiting for. My body tenses but Sawyer feels it. He delivers a slap to my ass, then squeezes the sting away.

"Relex, firefly. Let us fuck you up and love good you afterward," he murmurs. "I want to make you ours forever."

I moan and spread my legs uselessly, knowing he won't take my pussy anyway.

Sawyer laughs and pats my empty hole, then pulls his fingers free and fills my ass with his cock.

I scream around Beau's length, the sound muffled as he thrusts deep. Once, then again. He holds me there, his hand cupped to the back of my head as he pulses forward. I choke, knowing he won't let me up as Sawyer rails my ass.

A tongue drags over my pussy, laving the swollen, dripping flesh. Then my clit that throbs in need. I rock against Cody's face, forgetting the need to breathe, the pain where Sawyer destroys me. Beau's dominance.

Forgetting everything, except the need to come.

Cody gives me that, and I scream, my throat constricting on Beau's cock where he impales me on his length.

I come, taking him with me.

Beau's roar fills my world, mingling with Sawyer's as their seed empties into my body. Heat and salt and flesh slap and jerk until the wave ends, and then—

We fall. Again.

THANK YOU
FOR READING

Thank you so much for reading THE MOUNTAIN MAN'S UNTAMED BRAT. Please leave a REVIEW.

Want to read that BUNKHOUSE SCENE that wears Eden out so well between her and the Winterfox Woods boys? READ the BONUS EPILOGUE for FREE here.

IF YOU WANT to read more mountain men of the twisted, damaged variety, please visit RECURVE RIDGE and meet the five men who heal a trauma-tized girl that they can't let escape.

ABOUT THE AUTHOR

Dove *Priest* is a dark romance author who writes surrounded by her collection of stuffies, including her fur babies. Her characters haunt her until their stories are told. She is a corset fanatic and has a closet collection of dark fairy-tale retellings.

DOVE HAS five other pen names but won't share them unless provided with black coffee.

WWW.SOFIAAVES.COM

Join Dove's newsletter and get a free story.

FOLLOW DOVE

Facebook
Instagram
Bookbub
Amazon

READ DOVE'S SERIES

Recurve Ridge
   The Mountain Men's Untamed Brat

Siren on the Range

Sundown on the Range

Spirit on the Range

Ash on the Range

Mistletoe on the Range (2025)

Forgotten Mountain Man

Texan Devils

Ranger's Wish

Ranger Bedevilled

Ranger's Passion

Ranger's Fury

Ranger's Wrath

Ranger's Storm

Snapdragons & Seductions

Summer with a Ranger

Merry with a Ranger

Beach Duty Collection

Playing to Win

Off Boarding

Vicious Slash

Zero Pointer

Off Stage Fling

Rippton Allstars

Crushing It

Glacial Force

Rippton Creatives

Study Games

Make Me, Break Me

Twisted Obsession

Spring Break with a Mafia Prince

A Royally Fake French Menage

Angel Shot

Jericho Chimeras

Puck Me Always

Puck My Heart

Puck me Sideways

Z Boys

King

Joker

Hearts

Ace

Mayhem & Mistletoe

Ruski

Fast Track to Love

Speed Trap

Klauss Brothers

Zander

Keegan

Gallo Empire *with Jade Marshall*

Splintered Vows

Fractured Vows

Fierce Vows

Savage Covenant

. . .

Rom Coms

    She's A Hot Christmas Mess

    Boats, Moats and Root Beer Floats

Writing Romantasy as

    SOFIA SHELLEY

    Dead Poets Sorority

Kidlit writing as

    JO SEYSENER

    The OCD Elf

    The OCD Elf's Great Reindeer Calamity

    Greg and the Egg

writing YA as

    JOSS PHOENIX

    Alchem Academy

    HIDE FROM US

Writing spicy paranormal romance as

    RAVEN HUSH

    Club Fray

    Darkest Desires

Purge

Kidnapped By Claws

Ruin

Shadow Lords

Sinner's End

Heaven's Gate (2026)

Monster Brides

Phoenix's Eternal Flame

Kraken's Vow

Krampus' Christmas Bride

Silent Sentinels Duet

Reflections of Silence

Echoes in the Void

Monsters In New York

Feral Moon Rising

Dark Water Refuge